Gutter Governor

El Digger

Spreader

El Plantador

Fertilizer

Pew!

El Edger

Power Washer

Super Sodder

LEAF PileDriver

JESÚS TREJO

PAPÁ'S MAGICAL WATER-JUG CLOCK

Pictures by
ELIZA KiNKZ

minerva

BUENOS DÍAS!

Finally, it's Saturday—the day I get to help Papá at work!

Papá's a gardener.
I like to plant, cut grass,
and trim trees too. I especially
love all the tools we get
to use.

This is our family business,
and we make a great team!

Mamá

Papá

Jesús

In the kitchen, I fill Papá's big water jug.

"You know, Jesús, this is no ordinary water jug," Papá says.

"It's also a magical clock. It tells us how much work is left to do! When the jug is empty, that means, time to go home."

Mamá packs our lunch with love and says,
"It's going to be a hot one, mijo!"

As she heads out the door to her own job, Mamá calls, "Remember to drink lots of agua."

Papá loads our mighty work van with all the tools and machines.

When he yanks open the rusty sliding door, a smell of oil, gasoline, and yesterday's cut grass comes whooshing out.

We put the water-jug clock in the front seat with me, so I can make sure it doesn't tip over and spill.

Off we go, with the tools all rattling like a happy kind of music behind us. Even the water-jug clock sloshes to the beat.

The Saldañas' house is
stop número uno.

The Saldañas have a neat little house,
a big rose garden, and a bunch of super-old cats.
Our job is to water their roses and tidy up their yard.

I mow the lawn

and Papá edges it to make it look nice and crisp.

I'm starting to feel a little bit tired
from all this work, so I get me and
Papá each a cup of water.

I take another cup
to splash on my face.

Juan Diego's house is **stop número dos.**
It is much bigger than the Saldañas'.

A tiny dog lives here too.

Papá goes to work trimming the leaves at the top of the tall, tall, spooky trees. They kind of look like long, skinny monsters.

But I ignore them and go back to trimming the scary leaves at the bottom.

Woof!

This is **A LOT** of work! I go and get me and
Papá each another cup of water. And two
more cups to splash on my face.

Woof!

WOOF!!

Already, the water in the magical water-jug clock is half gone!
At this rate, we'll be home in no time.
Papá and I are such a good team, Mamá would be proud!

Stop número tres is the Márquez family's house.
It's the biggest one of them all. Today there's something
new on the huge front lawn . . . peacocks!

Papá uses the weed wacker to get rid
of all the small weeds,

and I use my little shovel to pick the
bigger weeds out by the root.

Now I'm **really** tired from all this work, so I get Papá and me each another cup of water.

And **uno,**

dos,

tres more cups to splash on my face.

"Nice dance moves!" says Papá.

"Yeah," I say. "Thanks, Papá!"

"You better go inside and ask to use the bathroom," he says.

Whoa . . . how did he know? Is Papá a psychic?!

Back outside, I get busy trimming and raking the leaves. Then I notice something important.

"What happened to all the agua?"
Papá says.

"The magic worked!
Let's see. You drank three cups.
I drank three big cups. I splashed a lot on my face."

"Oh! And there were the super-old cats,
and that thirsty dog in the sweater."

"And the poor peacocks with their heavy tails!"

"Now that the jug is empty, it's time for us to go home and rest."

Papá shakes his head. "Mijo, it's only 10:30 in the morning, and we still have eleven more houses to do before the workday is over. It's not time to go home, at all."

OH NO! Where did I go wrong?

Did I break the magical water-jug clock?

Did I maybe use too much water, too fast?

I hang my head.

I know I was in charge of the water-jug clock and I tried my best to do everything right.

We go sit under a tree.

"The water jug isn't really a magical clock," Papá says.
"We can't go home just because it's empty.
It's a plain old jug, mijo."

Papá sighs. "You're my partner, but you're also my kid.
That's why I try to make our workday fun.
This job, our family business, is hard, hard work.
But work is easier when you can play and
have fun at the same time."

"But now we have no water
left, and we have eleven more
houses. I feel bad." I say.

Papá, are you going to fire me from the family business?

"No, mijo, not even a little," Papá says.
"We will just fill it up again."

Okay. I can help with that. I go inside and ask to refill the jug.

Papá smiles.

We work hard the rest of the day.
We do all eleven houses, and I am a big help.

I am careful with
the water jug.

I don't drink more than I need,
or serve drinks to any animals,

or splash too much water on my face anymore.

Time and water are precious.

We don't want to waste them.

Papá and I find other ways to make the workday fun.

I make Papá laugh by telling him the silly
things I'm thinking about.

When our water jug is empty again, it really is time to go home.

It was a very good Saturday.
We worked, we sang, we laughed.
WE ARE A MAGICAL TEAM.

Dedicated to my loving parents.
¡Los quiero mucho! —JT

For my dad, who always got me queso —EK

An imprint of Astra Books for Young Readers, a division of Astra Publishing House
astrapublishinghouse.com
Printed in China

ISBN: 978-1-6626-5104-5 (hc)
ISBN: 978-1- 6626-5105-2 (eBook)
Library of Congress Control Number: 2022901205

First edition, 2023

10 9 8 7 6 5 4 3 2 1

Design by Amelia Mack
The text is set in Beanstalker.
The speech bubbles are hand lettered by Eliza Kinkz.
The illustrations are done with pencil, ink, watercolor, gouache,
crayons, and a few drops of queso.

Gutter Governor

El Digger

El Spreader

El Plantador

Fertilizer

El Edger

Power Washer

Super Sodder

LEAF PileDriver